The
Shape
of You

The Shape of You

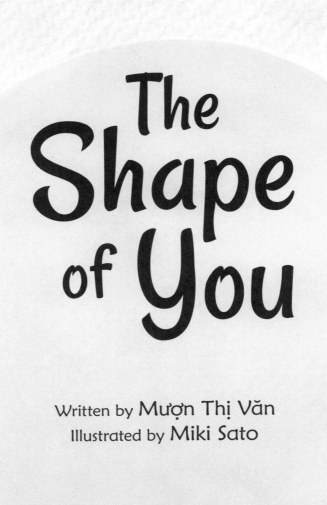

Written by **Mượn Thị Văn**
Illustrated by **Miki Sato**

Kids Can Press

The shape of the Earth
is a sphere.

But from any side,
it looks like a circle.

We live on this side,
on a hill
shaped like a triangle.

The shape of our door
is a rectangle.

The shape of our table
is a square.

The shape of this water
is a cup,
but sometimes it's a cube

or a cloud.

The shape of light
    is all the colors of the sunset —

red, yellow, blue,
   tangerine, chartreuse, mulberry, too.

The shape of order
is numbers —

ones you can count up to,

and ones you can't.

The shape of thinking
is quiet.

The shape of learning
is a question.

The shape of surprise is best when it hides what's inside.

The shape of the wind
is a scarf flapping.

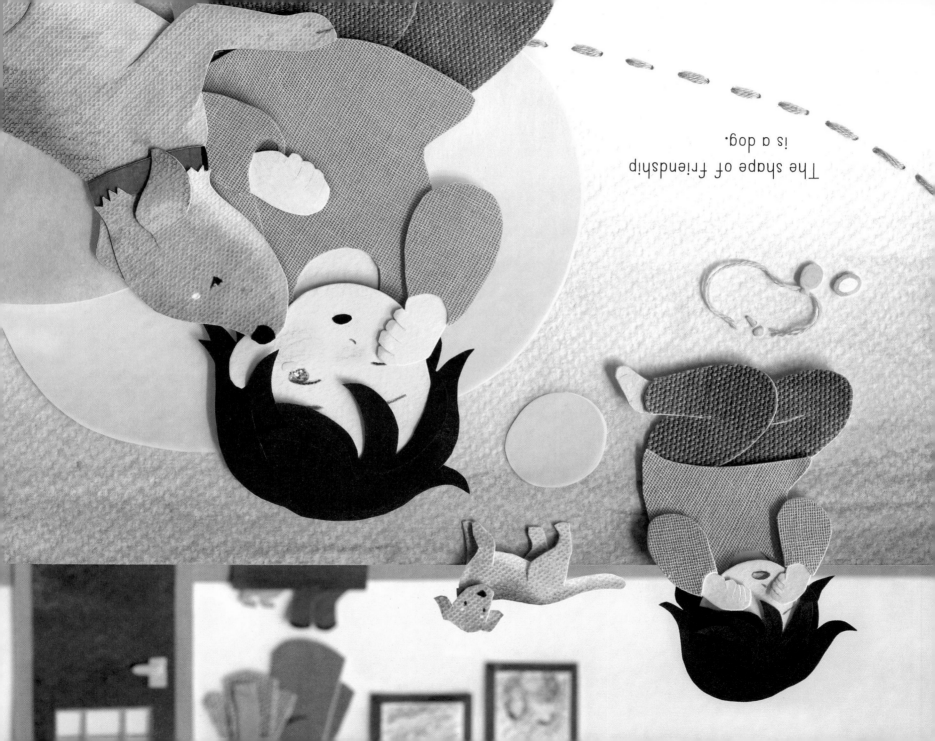

The shape of friendship
is a dog.

The shape of warmth
   is a space waiting to be filled.

The shape of a good story
wraps around tight.

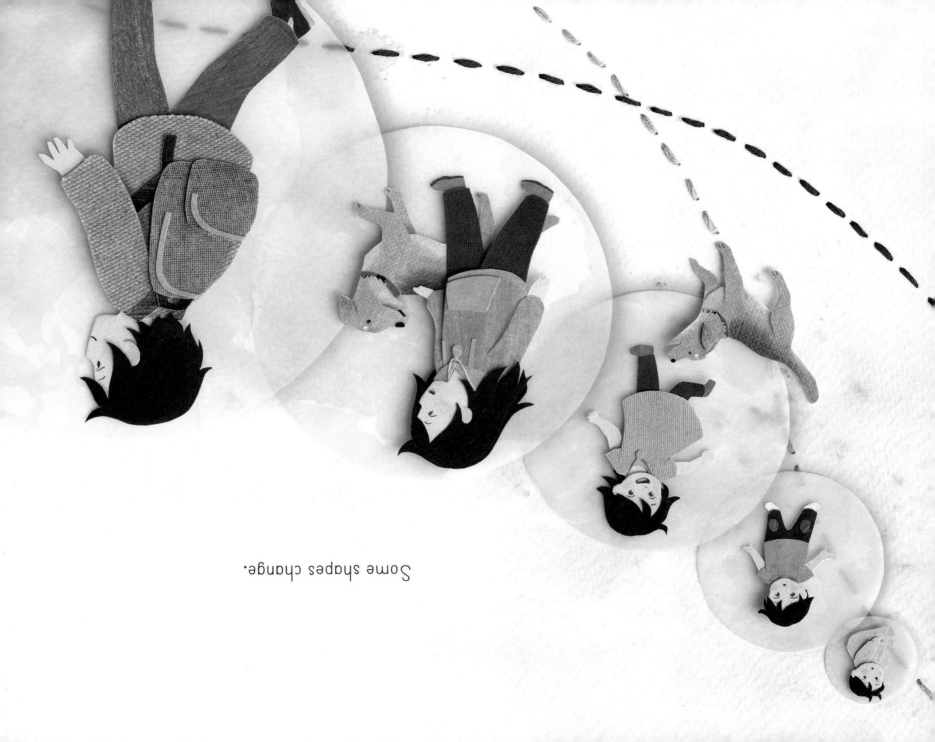

Some shapes change.

But some remain the same.

The shape of my fingers
will always fit yours.

And the shape of my love
will always be you.

Published in Canada and the U.S. by Kids Can Press Ltd.
25 Dockside Drive, Toronto, ON M5A 0B5

Kids Can Press is a Corus Entertainment Inc. company

www.kidscanpress.com

The artwork in this book was created with collage paper, textiles and embroidery thread.
The text is set in Catalina Clemente.

Edited by Yasemin Uçar and Sarah Howden
Designed by Michael Reis

Printed and bound in Malaysia in 10/2022

CM 23 0 9 8 7 6 5 4 3 2 1

MIX
Paper from responsible sources
FSC® C005748

Library and Archives Canada Cataloguing in Publication

Title: The shape of you / written by Mượn Thị Văn ; illustrated by Miki Sato.
Names: Van, Muon, author. | Sato, Miki, 1987- illustrator.
Identifiers: Canadiana 20220237972 | ISBN 9781525305450 (hardcover)
Classification: LCC PZ7.1.V36 Sha 2023 | DDC j813/.6 — dc23

Kids Can Press gratefully acknowledges that the land on which our office is located is the traditional territory of many nations, including the Mississaugas of the Credit, the Anishnabeg, the Chippewa, the Haudenosaunee and the Wendat peoples, and is now home to many diverse First Nations, Inuit and Métis peoples.

We thank the Government of Ontario, through Ontario Creates; the Ontario Arts Council; the Canada Council for the Arts; and the Government of Canada for supporting our publishing activity.